Nothi

NOTHING BUT THE RAIN

NAOMI SALMAN

A TOM DOHERTY ASSOCIATES BOOK

NEW YORK

This is a work of fiction. All of the characters, organizations, and events portrayed in this novella are either products of the author's imagination or are used fictitiously.

NOTHING BUT THE RAIN

Copyright © 2023 by Naomi Salman

Cover images by Nadav Kander / Trunk Archive
Cover design by Christine Foltzer

A Tordotcom Book
Published by Tom Doherty Associates/Tor Publishing Group
120 Broadway
New York, NY 10271

www.tor.com

Tor* is a registered trademark of Macmillan Publishing Group, LLC.

The Library of Congress Cataloging-in-Publication Data
is available upon request.

ISBN 978-1-250-84980-9 (paperback)
ISBN 978-1-250-84981-6 (ebook)

First Edition: 2023

For Sharron, who came from space
and flung me into the stars

I

1.

Found a notebook at long last. Bottom drawer in my ex-husband's study. Should have thought to look there earlier. Maybe I just didn't want to. Tried to think of a title for this whole thing, then dismissed that as silly. This isn't going to be *The Diary of Laverne Gordon*. This entry isn't even Day One. I'm long past believing I can keep track of days, so numbers it'll be. And if you're reading this, go to hell. I'm not writing this for posterity. I'm writing this for myself. God knows I'm sure to need an account of my own thoughts soon.

2.

I'm glad I have this journal now, because I couldn't keep writing on the walls, but I really wish it hadn't made me go inside Charlie's study. Now I can't stop thinking about him. I fought so hard to keep this house—my childhood home—and kick him out of Aloisville altogether; at the time, it felt like such an incredible victory, after months of tearing each other apart over every single one of our joint possessions. Isn't that ironic? Got exactly what I wanted, didn't I? I do hope Charlie's laughing at me wherever he is. Or maybe worrying about me. Who knows. The first option's more likely. Either way, it would mean he's alive and well, and things aren't the same where he is. That would almost be comfort enough.

3.

Aloisville used to be rainy when I was a child, and if anything it's only gotten worse. Even in the summer we get a serious downpour every couple of days, interspersed with light showers by way of a reprieve, and some medium drizzling to tie it all together. I think we're in the fall now. It's pouring day in and day out.

4.

Rain drumming on the roof. I never really cared for that sound. Can't understand why some people find it soothing. All this talk of white noise and sophrology and feeling close to nature. Well, now we're all starting to remember why most of history can be summed up as one long struggle to get away from it. If it was only rain I wouldn't have reason to complain, or not as much. The water's one thing; what it's doing to us is another. Only good side to this mess is that nobody can shoot me looks anymore when I grumble about that cursed noise. They all hate the rain now. Bully for me.

5.

Awake again. Always seem to wake up to that sound. It's much lighter today, almost fading in the background, but not quite. This quieter patter on the shingles is like an evil whisper right out of a horror movie. I can never make out any actual words—I'm not *that* kind of crazy old lady—but some days I'd almost like that better. We'd all give a lot to get some answers.

6.

I say *today* and *yesterday* but I'm not even sure what day it is. Our phones all went dark a while ago. I mean, you can still get them to light up, even use the apps, but there's absolutely no service, no GPS, no Internet, to the point that they don't display the time. Let alone the date. They factory reset every time you turn them on. I didn't even know such a thing was possible. Now I wish I'd been more frivolous in my retirement and bought one of those expensive analog watches, the kind that gives you the time, the date, and the phase of the goddamn moon without the help of a satellite. And, of course, nobody remembers the day this whole nightmare started. That's a day we *all* forgot. We didn't know to be careful yet. All taken by surprise, we must have been. Probably went for groceries, didn't bother with an umbrella since it's always raining, got to the store and forgot what to buy. Or maybe went out to walk the dog in the rain, and forgot the dog's name. Forgot the dog was even ours. Must have happened over and over again, layers and layers of amnesia, forgetting that we were forgetting at all. And so we went in a daze through blurry, shapeless days, before we finally began to realize there was something in the water.

7.

Now I'm thinking about dogs left out in the rain. Does it affect dogs? It'd be easy to know. Tie them up outside, leave them out for a bit, go back out after a shower and see if they still perk up when you tell them *heel*. All I had was a cat, apparently, a tiny orange kitten—and it's much harder to tell with cats, isn't it? For all we know, they don't *have* any long-term memory, only instinct and smells to find their way home every day. I mean, all they do is sleep, and they don't answer when you call their name, and they don't always realize when there's food in their bowl. Anyway, I probably didn't have that kitten long, because I forgot I even had her and turned her into roadkill when I tried backing the car out of the garage. I was so upset that I left the engine running while I picked up the little body, and then forgot about the car entirely, as soon as the wind blew a few drops of rain inside. So now I have no gas and the battery's dead. Just like the poor cat.

There was a little bowl of cat food in the garage. The kitten really must have been mine. I wish I knew her name. I wish I knew who gave her to me. I buried her in the backyard and just left the car outside. Who cares? It's got blood on the tires. And it won't start.

8.

When I ask myself what's the oldest thing I can recall, I have no right answer. I remember my name, and my childhood, and my ex-husband, and plenty other things. But in between these old solid times and our shitshow of a present, there's a whole lot of cognitive quicksand. You can't tell where it starts or where it ends. Sometimes I'm positive I can trace the shape of this hole in my life; and then I realize I can remember something that might have happened before, or after, or even during, and the line shifts again. I dream of that hole at night. A blank continent burned right through the map. I don't even remember how it feels, to know things for sure. We used to take our memory for granted; we didn't care that we couldn't recall what we'd eaten for breakfast four days ago, or the name of our math teacher in middle school. Now it's the most crucial issue in existence. If you don't know every single detail of your own life, how can you be sure you know anything at all?

9.

Beans. From a can, heated up on the stove. My breakfast, for future reference. That's not four days ago, that's today. Whatever day it is.

10.

I do remember the first thing I wrote, and I don't mean here in this journal. I'm talking about the day I finally understood what was happening, when I lost my last little bits of doubt and denial. I remember my panic, I remember that I scrambled to write it down somewhere, get it out of my mind before it could be erased—I didn't know what was happening or how long the effect lasted, I didn't yet know the rain couldn't chase me inside the house—I turned over the whole living room for something to write with, found an old felt-tip pen that still worked but no notebook, no paper, no flyers and no books, no nothing—didn't cross my mind to check Charlie's study at the time, I was so sure the clock was ticking—so I ended up scrawling it across the wall out of sheer panic.

SOMETHING IN THE WATER.

Didn't cover it up even after I'd calmed down, hours later. Because why should I? Charlie didn't have the best taste, so it's actually an improvement. Gives this bland house some personality. And that way, it's the first thing I see when I get home, right above the coat rack. I'm sure never to forget it again. Gotta keep track of what's important, right? So I kept on writing more and more. My house is like my brain now: I can walk in my mind. YOUR NAME IS LAVERNE. YOUR BIRTHDAY IS JANUARY 19TH. Of course, I wrote these factoids before I understood how it all worked. Now I know for sure I'm not losing my name anytime soon, which is always a comfort. It could happen, but if I lose that it means I've lost everything else, and there won't be enough of me left to worry about what happens next.

11.

MILITARY BLOCKADE is the second biggest thing I wrote. (Kitchen wall, nice plaster with good texture; felt-tip dries quick, smell doesn't last long, and the black ink is shockingly stark against the white paint. You can't miss it.) Sometime later—you can tell by the difference in how the words are faded—I added ALL AROUND TOWN, and underlined it twice. Must have done a bit of additional reconnaissance. Shame I don't remember it. Now you try telling me the Army ain't involved.

12.

It might not be the Army. Truth is, we have no idea what's going on. After I was done scribbling my panic in all caps I calmed down and wrote out possible explanations for what's been happening. Naturally aliens are on the list, right next to the rapture, the apocalypse, and sleeping with my phone under my pillow. (They all used to say it wasn't good for your health.) I've also considered that maybe none of this is happening and I've just gone insane. It's actually my most comforting hypothesis. But it'd be one hell of a long-lasting, not to mention freakishly coherent delusion—the whole town in on it, too. No, can't buy it. Right now, the theory I'm favoring is military neurochemicals that were field-tested a bit too early. Got out of control, drifted to civilian territory, seeped into the earth and clouds. And the rest was history.

Wouldn't even be the first time. I remember a time the rivers turned burgundy for a week, and if you drank the water you went raving mad like a bat with rabies. Now *that* was trending for a while on the local news. Headlines all said LET MY PEOPLE GO! along with other Old Testament jokes, because those are always hilarious. But there wasn't a blockade when the river went red. Nobody tried to keep information from getting out. It was just a chemical leak, easily explained and easily resolved, and the effects weren't even permanent. I'm certain of all this, because it all happened way back when I was a kid, so it'd take me quite some time standing in the rain for that particular memory to wash away.

That's how it works—in retrograde. A droplet's all it takes for confusion to set in. You lose your days as if they were melting off, going further and further into your past. Little sugar dolls left in the rain, that's what we are now. If you're not careful, you'll melt all the way down to the infant inside. And if *she* melts away, you're done. Can't form new memories; I suppose you forget how. So now you're just an empty shell wandering around, until eventually you starve to death.

13.

The rain's not the only enemy. Puddles work too. I've done a lot of experiments in my spare time, even though chemistry wasn't my strong suit in college. I've been careful to write them all down on the walls, keeping track of minutes and seconds, because I've gotten a tad paranoid about timing myself. I'm too lazy to copy them all here; they're just strings of numbers with no real importance. But the experiments themselves were pretty straightforward and yielded some definite results. Got some rainwater in a glass, put an apple in a box. Pinned a note on the box with a question: *There's an apple in the box. What color is it?* Then I dipped my finger in the rainwater, just a touch. That took guts, let me tell you. According to my notes I psyched myself up for five minutes before I found the courage to do it the first time.

It was a peculiar sensation. Like losing your train of thought—only I lost all my trains of thought at once. Stared into space, blinked. *What was I thinking about?* With an effort, I remembered I was doing an experiment, but when my eyes fell on the paper, I couldn't answer my own question. I wrote that down. You have to write it all down. Then I tried again. And again and again, until at last the water stopped wiping my memory when I touched it. Two hours, thirteen minutes and twenty-six seconds—it's circled in heavy red marker on the wall; that's how long it takes for whatever's in the water to evaporate. I knocked back the whole glass to celebrate, and I could still remember the apple's color afterwards. Still remember it now. Red with a bit of yellow. And the relief I felt when I realized we weren't going to die of thirst.

14.

I did the rounds to tell everyone my discovery. Ain't I an upstanding citizen? I may be an old misanthrope living away from town, but I did use to be a doctor, and it felt wrong to leave people in the dark, cowering inside their houses and slowly dying of dehydration because they were afraid the rainwater might seep into the pipes. (Which, for the record, it does.) An old fart like me shouldn't have to do this, but desperate times don't care about your bad hip. I printed two hundred instruction sheets with my findings, wrapped myself tight in clothing and duct tape until I damn near couldn't breathe, and then went out and walked all over town, braving the rain, putting a copy in every mailbox. Felt like some sort of apocalyptic Jehovah's Witness. Went from house to house until I was all out. I didn't cover the whole town, let alone the whole neighborhood, but I still did my part. Nobody's come to thank me, but I do like to think I saved a few lives. Brought a semblance of peace to a few minds.

Or maybe someone else had figured it out before me and I made a fool of myself. Well, I'm at peace with my conscience, and that's what matters.

15.

More on those water experiments, because I realize I never did write down the rest of my results in here. If I'm going to treat this journal as my backup brain, might as well do it right. I don't want to lose my mind on some unlucky day and then curse myself for not writing the one detail I shouldn't have left out.

So: the rain needs to settle for over two hours before it

becomes plain old boring water. Volume of water has no influence on the time it takes for whatever's in it to stop working; boiling or freezing it doesn't change a thing either. Proves it's not some bacterial or viral agent. Like I said—chemicals. Which means the military quarantine's bullshit, but I could have figured that one out without any fancy experiments. I'm certain the reason for the quarantine isn't so the outside world won't get contaminated; it's so *we* can't get the word *out*. Some people out there are mighty embarrassed by what they've done, I'd bet my house on it.

Now, I wouldn't mind a nondisclosure agreement if it meant I could leave this goddamn town. But nobody seems interested in having me sign one. According to my wallpaper, you can try shouting at the guards on the military posts around the city, but they don't listen. All you'll get is a warning shot. Again: assuming they are the Army. I just know they have guns. Those people don't even look human, with their gas masks and their black rubber outfits like deep sea divers.

16.

They *could* be aliens.

17.

Or maybe we're at war and it's actually a hostile army. Or maybe *they* forgot too much and they think *we're* the aliens. Or maybe this is hell.

So much for trying to be less crazy.

18.

If I'm not mistaken I have to go see Katie Rathbone tomorrow. Thrilling times.

19.

The real issue for us survivors here in Aloisville is food. We've got water, we've even got power—and if we've got power then *everybody knows we're here,* so why hasn't anybody come to help?—but food is bound to become an issue. I can't think of a way out of here. Nobody can. We could take to the streets, but we'd forget what we were doing mid-riot. Or the guards would gun us all down, and the survivors would lose their minds trying to crawl away under the drizzle. It really does rain all the time, or nearly so. Greenest country you've ever seen—there's some goddamn upside to the situation. At least it means we can grow our own food, except nobody's really gotten around to it yet, as far as I can tell. I did plant some cabbages and carrots in my backyard, half-heartedly. Forgot about them for a while; only remembered them when I saw a note scrawled above my bathroom mirror. Went out to check and found the earth still freshly turned. Not one green shoot poking out. How long had it been? I don't know. Maybe I only planted them three days ago. Or maybe I'm just that bad at gardening. Anyway, my pantry's still full, and I know I haven't been forgetting to eat even when I forget other things. So, really, it can't have been that long since the amnesia rains started.

20.

The motherfuckers are airdropping us food. I must have known it once and then forgot. I just wrote it across my kitchen wall in a fit of fury right after I dragged the damn bag in. Then I remembered I have the journal now, so I'm also writing it here. AIRDROPPED BAG OF FOOD. IS WHOLE TOWN EXPERIMENT? MOTHERFUCKERS! It feels even better to scrawl profanity than to yell it at the sky. Idiot thing nearly brained me. And I couldn't even see the chopper through the clouds. It's dangerous to look up for too long in Aloisville even with your face completely covered.

The bag is solid oilcloth with industrial stitches. I couldn't find a mark on it to say where it came from, and

God knows I turned the damn thing inside out and back again. The food is all nonperishable items, peas and beans and dried meat and powdered milk. Sealed bottles of water. All regular brands, could have come out of my grocery bags. Wait 'til Katie Rathbone hears about this—except she won't, not today. It's a narrow window that allows me to go see her and then come back before dark. I completely missed it, what with this whole bag-of-food-trying-to-flatten-me business.

I stored everything in my cupboards because I'm a hungry old woman who really does hate gardening. Then I got paranoid again and ran one of the cans through my regular amnesia tests, bean by goddamn bean. As far as I can tell, they're not contaminated. The whole thing took me so long that I was hungry again by the time I was done. So I ate another can to celebrate, without checking this time. Hope that wasn't a mistake. But even if it was, I couldn't tell now, since I'm writing all of this after the fact. Isn't *that* reassuring!

21.

Been thinking about this bag of food all night. What I really hate about it is that it's messing up my projected timeline. Up until now I was pretty sure it couldn't have been more than two months since it all started, tops. But now . . . now I don't know. Oh God. Maybe it's been years. How could we know for sure? How could we *know?*

22.

And of course it's raining again. I can hear it right now. I should really sleep somewhere other than the attic, but what can I do? Push my bed down the stairs? I'm sixty-three and I live alone. The couch in the living room would throw my back out. If only the aliens would airdrop some earplugs, that'd be real nice of them.

23.

Can't sleep. But that's fine. Heavy things falling from the sky is something I'd love to remember the next time I'm walking around town. So I need to make sure the memory won't fade away that easy. Let it burrow a few hours deep in the brain. Repeat it to myself over and over again.

24.

Still can't sleep, which I just wrote is a good thing. Except I'm bored to death, and hating my own thoughts, and there's nothing to do in here anymore. The TV doesn't work, there's no Internet, and I don't have that many books.

All my crosswords and sudoku are done, and of course I did them in ballpoint pen so I can't erase and redo them. All I can do is write and write, even though I'm running out of theories. My lists have taken over the walls. Could it really be aliens? Are we in their lab? That just sounds insane, but even the military theory starts to sound insane when I think too hard about it. Do you know what the most likely theory is? This is just what the weather does now. This is how the rain is. This is how things are; now, everywhere, and forever.

I mean, it would make more sense for the whole water cycle to be affected. Right? This ain't no surplus red paint in the river, gone after a couple of days. I'm talking about something that falls from the sky. Something that's born in the clouds. Which means it must have gone worldwide. Is that why our phones won't give us the time of day— because there are no more satellites to tell them? Are the Army rapture lab aliens really the last survivors of a memory apocalypse? Are they trying to help the rest of the world in whatever way they can? Are they too scared to ever come out of their rubber suits? Are the blockades here to protect us from something out there—something even *worse*?

I go spiraling like that, and then I remember that we have power, we have running water, which means things out there can't be *that* dire. You'd think it would be enough to calm me down for good, but it's actually rinse and repeat— so to speak—every other day. God, maybe the rain doesn't give you amnesia at all. Maybe it just makes you crazy.

25.

Or maybe I'm on the goddamn *Truman Show*.

26.

I just said I was running out of theories, but you know what? I'm not running out of ink. My ballpoint pen is full, and my felt-tip hasn't stopped working, either. Every wall has been written on at least once, but there's still a lot of room left; they don't look anything like the walls of those horrible prison cells in the movies, where the psychopath's been locked up and killed time by scribbling VENGEANCE again and again, using his own blood in overlapping paragraphs of insanity. My craziness hasn't taken over yet. So it *can't* have been that long. Unless they're airdropping stationary, too, and cleaning my walls while I'm not looking.

Tell you what, if I find a bag of office supplies in the street on my next outing, I'll just lie down in the mud and give up.

27.

The rain's stopping, for a change. All right. Enough eye straining. I'll try getting a bit of sleep before dawn.

28.

Morning's come at long last. Isn't it funny how these entries are getting more and more linear? This started out as a jumbled mess of instructions to navigate the death traps of Aloisville, and to rebuild myself from the ground up in case I melted too much in the rain. Writing a diary wasn't my plan, and yet now it seems to be writing itself. Guess I'm that starved for any kind of continuity.

I have to admit it's reassuring to reread and retrace. I can verify I haven't lost even a minute of my life to the rain. Which isn't hard, really, since I didn't go out at all. Well, except for that short-lived trip yesterday, with the food bag.

Speaking of which. I'm writing this at the kitchen table now, while I'm waiting for Katie. She's bound to come visit today, because I didn't go to see her yesterday like I was supposed to. Them's the rules: if your buddy doesn't come to the rendezvous point, you have to go check up on them the next day. I am the buddy and I didn't make rendezvous, so now I must sit and wait to be checked up on.

I could go *now,* meet her halfway, but I've learned the hard way that without a phone to agree on things from a distance, it's better to stay where you are and wait to be found. Just like when you're lost in the woods. Otherwise you look for each other all day, and your windbreaker feels like the flimsiest spider web in the world, and your scarf might as well be made out of toilet paper, and it's raining so *much,* and it's not stopping, and all that mind bleach moisture is getting into your lungs like nerve gas, and you end up running back home, and throwing up with panic, and stress, and shame, because you've potentially left someone else's mind to dissolve out there, just because you were too afraid for yourself.

I'm not doing that again, thanks. I'm waiting for Katie. Them's the rules.

29.

So why go out at all, you probably wonder? Why not just stay inside forever and ever? Well, you'd think rain is an easy thing to avoid when you've got a roof over your head, but it turns out we can't just stay inside all day. Not even in the middle of the apocalypse. *Especially* not in the middle of the apocalypse. Aloisville was a small town to start with, and there's fewer than two hundred of us now, if I'm counting right. Not to mention we're still losing people every once in a while, in a slow trickle. (Not the best choice of words. But I'm not striking out anything or I'll go mad trying to reconstruct the words in case I ever lose the memory of what they were.)

Enough with the rambling, Laverne, you'll wish you could kick your own ass on the reread. I meant to write about the buddy system we set up. Old age and retirement couldn't get me to agree to a minder; it took a damn amnesia plague to change my mind. At first, neighbors banded together to check on each other, but we realized what a mistake *that* was when we lost a whole pocket of people up on Baistach Hill. Fancy gated neighborhood where they all got hit at the same time, none of them self-aware enough to realize the others had gotten rained on. Fifty people, all gone, bit by bit. *Drop by drop.* Most of them died before anyone thought to check; the rest we had to mercy kill. They'd been forgetting to eat; they looked like walking skeletons. There were children. Families.

The ones who found them came to get me. Banged on my door calling my name. For a wild moment of stupid hope, I thought I was being rescued. I thought it was all over. Turns out it was Dave Logan and his neighborhood watch, still in operation somehow on the other side of Armageddon, saying they needed a doctor. But not to fix a broken arm or deliver a baby or any of that life-affirming crap. I'm the one they came to get; I'm the one who got to euthanize people. Because what were we going to do? Take them out back and shoot them? What a lovely way to spend my Sunday afternoon, right after thinking—for a minute there—that it was all over.

Now I've got no morphine left. Probably for the best.

I wish I could forget Baistach Hill, but instead I've marked down the days since it happened. It's all I have by way of a calendar, even though I probably forgot to mark it on some days, or forgot I'd already done so and marked it twice on others. Whatever the actual number should be, there are currently thirty-three notches under the huge

REMEMBER BAISTACH HILL that I have on the wall facing my bed. Should have done that as soon as I started writing on the walls, right? I just didn't think of it. Didn't realize then how hard it would be to keep track of days. Anyway, those thirty-three notches mean Baistach Hill happened at least a month ago, give or take. I'd have to stand in the rain for a long while before a whole month of my life went away. Can't afford to lose that much. Can't afford to forget what happened in Baistach Hill, lest it happen again.

Katie's still not here, which makes me real anxious, so I may as well keep going. Now, in our small post–Baistach Hill world, we have buddies across town instead of just nearby. Which means we have to trek through the rain to go check up on them. If it sounds counterintuitive and dangerous, well, that's because it really really is. But all the same, that's what works best. Once every two weeks, I have to go check on Katie Rathbone who lives alone with her child. And once every two weeks, she comes to check on me. Now, inevitably we mess up a lot, since we're all a little fuzzy on time; it's entirely possible she'll be more than a few hours late. One time I misjudged my own visit by two whole days. But at least we've been in the habit long enough that it can't be wiped from our minds so easily. I have her name carved right on the front door, inside and out. KATIE RATHBONE! KATIE RATHBONE! It helps her find my house whenever she gets scrambled in the head crossing town to come here.

She'll be coming to check on me today. I just have to wait

and not go out looking for her. I just have to wait. She'll be here soon.

30.

She's still not here, and I'm almost annoyed to be so damn worried about her. The funny thing is, Katie and I don't get along so well. It's not that we fight; we've just never really warmed up to each other. I'm an old harpy who's lived alone for the better part of the last decade, and she's a single mother that's a bit too prim and proper for my taste. But we've helped each other out a few times, and our buddy visits are holding strong. She's an electrician, which comes in handy around an ancient house like mine. As for her, she probably thought a doctor would be pretty useful to have nearby in the apocalypse; she seemed happy enough to pair up with me despite my less than sparkling personality. Except I'm retired and I don't have anything left by way of supplies, so there's very little I can do for people. Sorry to disappoint.

All the same, I try to be welcoming. Every time Katie visits me, I have a cup of hot water ready for her. She's showed me pictures of her little girl. Cute brown kid. Her name is

31.

Maisie
Millie
Zelie
Zadie
Chloe
Billie
Annie
Abby
Ellie

32.

Made a damn fool of myself. All because I couldn't remember the name of Katie's daughter. As soon as she came in—nobody knocks anymore; can't just stand out there in the rain—I jumped to my feet and started yelling at her. *What's her name? What's her name?* She looked baffled, standing there in her heavy rain gear, with that nameless kid in her arms. I can't believe she brought her along. She never has before, that I can remember. It's too dangerous out there for the toddlers, and she is barely more than a baby, that kid, looking at me with her big brown eyes. Never started crying, even though I must have frightened her with all my yelling. I have no patience, even less so when I'm afraid. Eventually, Katie understood what I was shouting and why, and she politely reminded me that the kid's name was Zoe. Of course. Zoe. And wouldn't you know it? I actually *did* remember that. I'd just forgotten, the way normal people forget normal things. I keep forgetting that's still possible. I keep forgetting about forgetting. So then I started to cry that I was going senile, I had dementia, I was no use to anyone and she should pair up with somebody else because I was going to die soon anyway—typical useless old lady rant, embarrassing everyone, completely pathetic. When Katie took off her gloves and gripped my hand to comfort me, her touch was a statement of fact. God, her plump young fingers on my stained wrinkled skin. I'd never felt so much shame in my life, not even the day I headed home thinking I'd left her to die somewhere in the rain. *You're not old, Laverne,* she kept saying. *You're only sixty-three!* Thirtysomething bitch.

Wasn't that just a lovely preamble. After I was done with my hysterics, Katie took off Zoe's little scarf and sat her at the table. As far as I could tell, she wasn't offended. Or she knew not to show it. I really should have remembered her daughter's name, but I suppose we all have other things on our minds. It's not the first time I've freaked out over forgetting such a small thing, either. But I usually have my panic attacks on my own time, so I can pretend later that nothing's happened. Really thought I'd age out of those, but if anything, they've gotten worse. Suppose the circumstances aren't helping. I've escaped to the bathroom now. I'm waiting for my hands to stop shaking. Keeping this goddamn diary calms me down. Streaming the old consciousness helps convince me I won't forget anything anytime soon. Won't make the same mistakes twice, not anymore. I want to remember everything, even my shame. Even my fear. It's not a good life, but it's my life. It's what I've got. I want it to stay inside my head.

At least I remembered to put some water in the fridge before Katie got here. You have to let it sit for over two hours before you can drink it. Three hours to be sure. Remember: even when it comes from the pipes. Nothing's safe. I'll heat it up in a saucepan and serve it to them in cups, like I always do. Wish I had some actual tea, but I don't. The air-droppers apparently don't consider tea an essential when filling their goddamn care packages.

All right. I've been in here for nearly fifteen minutes now. Can't hide in the bathroom any longer without Katie asking me if I've got stomach problems. And I'm feeling better anyway. Time to go back out and socialize. Lord. I've never liked people, I've always been fine on my own, and still am, even with everything that's happening. I wish we could just wave at each other from afar every week and then go on our merry way. That's my kind of buddy system.

33.

She's left Zoe with me. Has she lost her mind?

I was beginning to tell her about the airdropped food,

but she said she already knew—said that we'd actually found that out together, only two weeks before, when I came to visit her. Which means the rain wiped it from my memory as I made my way home. That's always wonderful to realize.

Before I even had time to digest that, she went on saying that she needed to go on a mission and I had to babysit her kid. Mission? What is she talking about? We're just soaking messes here, trying to survive day-to-day. When I asked her about it, she wouldn't give me any details. Said she didn't want to give me undue hope. Told her that was never a risk as far as I was concerned, but she still wouldn't say anything, just kept repeating I needed to take care of Zoe. And of course I said yes—I'm not happy about that, not happy at all, but what choice did I have? The buddy system is all that's left of organized society in Aloisville. I'm not even sure I understand why *Katie* would feel comfortable leaving her kid with me while she's off taking care of some mystery business. So now it's just Zoe and me, and I'm left thinking *what if something happens to her mother?* It would take a lot of rain for Katie to forget she has a daughter. But she could forget she's left her with me. Oh God. I should have made her write it down somewhere.

And that's avoiding the elephant in the room. What if something happens to *Zoe* while she's here? I don't know the first thing about taking care of children. At least she's a quiet, well-behaved kid who's content drawing on the walls of the crazy lady's house. Zoe doesn't say a word, which means she probably doesn't speak. Do kids her age usually speak? How old is she anyway? She's potty trained, and I've seen her toddle around from room to room, and her drawings aren't entirely abstract as far as I can tell, but those clues are no help to me and I can't just look it up online anymore. I was too embarrassed to ask Katie after I just forgot her daughter's name. So now she's gone and I'm left thinking about how horribly vulnerable this child is. I wasn't a pediatrician and I never had any children, which would be enough reason to panic. But then there's the rain.

Memories are the building blocks of children. They shape them every minute of every day. If they lose their immediate present, they don't have anything else to fall back on, not like us old crones. Zoe in Aloisville is like a sandcastle built too close to the sea. She's so small. Mere minutes in the rain might be enough to wipe out most of her, if not all of her. That thought is making my hands shake. How am I going to keep her clean? You can't just pop into the shower anymore. Water from the pipes isn't as bad as the rain, but it's bad enough. A lot of people on Baistach Hill were found naked and absent in their bathrooms, their souls gone down the drain while they weren't paying attention. I'd better draw a bath now, so I can let it sit long enough that it's not dangerous anymore. But then it'll be cold and the kid won't like that. How does Katie do it? I should have asked her these things. But she assumed I knew how to take care of a child, and I didn't tell her any different because I was too proud. She said she'd be back for Zoe in two days. I hope to God that's true.

34.

I ended up heating safe water on the stove and rubbing Zoe down with a washcloth. Same as what I do for myself. Then I made her some soup which she ate without too much fuss. It's strange that she doesn't make any noise. Aren't kids supposed to make a racket at this age? But Zoe's content to keep doodling on my walls and staring at her palms. Which means either she's seen something that's shocked her into silence, or forgotten it a bit too well. Who knows what Katie let happen to her before she realized what was happening. I won't be the one to question Katie on that. Nobody can be held accountable for the rain.

The kid's asleep now. She looks so much like me with her little cornrows, almost the exact same style as mine. Who does her hair? Is it Katie? Did she learn for her kid's sake? Or did someone else do it before this madness started? Here I am, trying to measure the passage of time by the neatness of a kid's hairdo. I just wish I knew for sure what day it was. Wish I knew what the hell's going on. At times I still think the rain *has* to be a natural phenomenon. But all the phones blacking out, that *must* have been deliberate. Right?

Again, I choose to find comfort in that. We wouldn't be shut away from the rest of the world if there was no more world. It's awful knowing you're in a cage, but it's better than fearing the cage might be all that's left.

35.

Slept horribly. Kept waking up to check on Zoe. I had the same dream all night—came back to it every time I managed to fall asleep, like someone was pausing a movie in my mind, waiting for me to return with stale popcorn and warm soda. I dreamed, of course, that she'd vanished and that I was looking for her, first in the kitchen where I found the tap running and the sink overflowing, then in the bathroom where I found the shower on and the tub filled to the brim, only to discover Zoe'd somehow managed to rip through the screen door and had been sitting playing in the rain.

But every time I went to check on her, she was fine, and I didn't once wake her, no matter how many times I brushed her hair with my fingertips to check that she was dry. In the end, she slept through the night in her nest of blankets, and I got out of bed for good before dawn. When I get up too early I usually feel like a pathetic old lady who can't sleep, but I was sick of drowning in my dreams. I'm watching the sunrise now.

Actual bit of blue sky this morning. Won't last for long, but for a few minutes there, that makes it seem like everything's all right.

36.

Sometimes I wish I could forget what's been happening. Then I remember that's what I'm most afraid of.

37.

Goddammit. What do kids eat for breakfast?

38.

Katie Rathbone's back and she's lost her damn mind. And I don't mean she walked bareheaded in the rain. That might've been for the better.

At least she came back, two days later just like she said, which was a relief. I immediately handed Zoe over, mumbled that she'd behaved just fine, and gave them both cups of hot water and the usual stale cookies. I never take a cookie for myself. At my age, it's probably better. We only had one dentist in town and he was among the people we lost on Baistach Hill. And everyone knows sugar's terrible for toddlers, so Katie shouldn't let Zoe nibble on those. But I don't tell people how to raise their own kids. Anyway, as soon as I started fixing my own cup of barely safe water, Katie began saying that her mission had been successful and we needed to talk. She said she was leaving town tomorrow, along with fifty other people, and she wanted me to come with them.

Just then I broke my cup in the sink. I swear it was a coincidence. I wouldn't lie to myself in my own diary. It slipped and it broke and I nearly cut myself, like an easily startled old lady with trembling hands. Except my hands don't shake, and I wasn't surprised. All I wanted to do was roll my eyes. This isn't the first time Katie's tried roping me into that kind of foolishness; didn't forget *that* about her, even though I never really wrote it down. (Well, not in so many words. There might be a few insults to her intelligence scribbled behind the foot of my bed where she won't see.) I've always managed to discourage her. So this time around, I just sighed and shook the shards of porcelain off my fingers and got another cup from the cupboard, and told her she was being an idiot. At my age, I can be as tactless as I want.

She retorted that there was a plan this time. Oh, well, if there's a *plan*!

Zoe was looking at me when I joined them at the table. I wonder who that kid's father is. There aren't many Black folk in Aloisville, and even though my memory isn't what it used to be, I'm pretty damn certain I never had children. Or grandchildren. But I say again, it's crazy how much that little girl looks like me. And her huge brown eyes. Little kids don't mind looking you in the eye for a long time, and I don't mind either when they do. It's almost soothing. Certainly easier than meeting Katie's tiny blue eyes, which kept trying to hold mine. Eventually I couldn't avoid them any longer, and I had to ask her what her goddamn plan was.

We'll go through the plastic streets to the southeast edge of town, all of us together, she said. Except the plastic streets aren't as safe as she thinks they are, which I didn't refrain from telling her. A few tarps stretched above narrow alleys? Come on. That is a recipe for disaster: sure, they shield you at first, but then they swell up with rain, tip over. You couldn't pay me to go there. She just smiled at me when I told her. Said obviously it wasn't perfect, but it would minimize the risks. All right, honey, whatever you say. Go through the plastic streets, see if I care. You'll hit the southeast blockade and the guards will shoot you down like fish in a barrel.

We still have running water. Still have electricity. We're being airdropped supplies. We're being kept alive for some reason. Katie can call me a paranoid old crank all she wants—even though she's never that impolite, especially not under my own roof—but my point is, we're fine as long as we stay within city limits. Try crawling out of the vivarium, though, and you'll be fed to a snake.

I told her all that and more. Zoe just listened and stared. Poor kid, I thought. Her mother's going to get her killed. Because of course Katie was undeterred. *We can get out if we've got something to hold against them!* She was all excited. *Dave Logan found one bar!* Dear Lord. A bar of gold would've been more exciting than what old Dave Logan actually found: one bar of cell service.

I'll admit I got a little shock hearing it. More proof the world's still there. Katie ranted on and on about the video they'd filmed, ready to go live, summing up everything—the amnesia rains, the military blockade, the quarantine. They probably have PowerPoint slides and a musical number to complete the package, bless them. *If they don't let us through, we'll upload it for everyone to see!* Goodness gracious, but she's stupid.

When I pointed out letting fifty people through amounted to the same thing, only way worse, she just stared at me as if I'd started barking at her.

Zoe was gnawing on her second cookie. I wanted to ask Katie if Dave Logan knew what day it was. What month. What year. But for some reason, I was almost embarrassed to ask, as if it were some stupid concern of mine alone. Before I could say anything, anyway, Katie took a deep breath and launched into one of her speeches. *Laverne, you're a good person,* and *I've come to like you in spite of our differences,* and also *I know you like your peace, but this isn't peace!* and more, *This is stillness! This is a cage! This is a death trap!* along with a side helping of *Don't you see? Don't you understand?* Me, I just drank my hot water. I agreed with everything she was saying, which was precisely the reason I didn't want to try getting out. Some people out there were very serious about keeping us in. I didn't want to make them mad. That was when she opened her little eyes as wide as they would go. *Will you come with us?*

Not a chance, honey. You're all going to get shot.

I told her as much. She stared at me for a long time. She didn't try arguing again. She left not long after that, and I'm not ashamed to say I didn't hold her back. You cannot save those who are beyond help; Baistach Hill taught me that, and I made sure the lesson would stick in my own mind at least. I'm sure Katie feels the same way about me, now.

I just wish I could stop thinking about Zoe. That child's not even old enough to speak, let alone understand what's going on. And I don't have the energy it would take to save her.

39.

Zoe. I wrote that name a hundred times on the walls, and I'm writing it again now on the page. I need to fix it in my mind. I want to remember her if she disappears. How she looked before she left. It's the least I can do. I'm afraid it's all I can do. What else could be done, really? Can't throw Katie out in the rain and steal her kid. God, I should be sleeping. This time, I have no reason to be up in the morning, but I just can't stop thinking about little Zoe, and about Katie Rathbone's plan. Part of me understands what she's going through. I've been going through the same thing. Part of me is angry at her for the judgment I saw in her eyes. Of course I wish I could leave, damn it! Of course I wish it would all stop and life would start making sense again!

I did consider killing myself, at the beginning, when I

barely knew what was happening and the fear was just too much. I even knew how I was going to do it—razor blade, sleeping pills, warm bath. Bit of leftover Novocain so there wouldn't even be any pain. The option's still open, but these days I'm more afraid of dying than living. Humans are weird, contrary creatures. One thing I never did consider, though, was killing other people. We all have a right to our own lives, even in the middle of madness, despair, and terror. We don't know for sure whether there's an afterlife; this one is all we have that's certain. Taking it away from someone else—that would be stealing, pure and simple. You can't solve people's unhappiness by ending their existence. You certainly can't do that when it's your own kid that's suffering. Is Zoe suffering? She is such a quiet, even-tempered child. She probably doesn't even remember a time when things were different. She could grow up in this strange bubble of a world, learning to avoid the rain like other girls were taught to avoid dark streets and men at night. She could yet live.

I keep thinking Katie knows her plan is suicide, and just doesn't care. But to the point of dragging her daughter down with her? There's got to be something I can do. I've never been one for kids, but I don't want to see that little one dead in a puddle of mind wipe. I've seen enough dead childr

40.

The kitchen lights just snapped off

41.

All right. Okay. Here is the situation. I tried turning them on again and it didn't work. Neither did the lamp in the hallway. Obviously, the fuses have blown. That's all right. I have some spares left. Found them without trouble. Holding them now. But the fuse box is in the basement and the basement is damp.

I do have a flashlight, thank God, and the batteries are full. I'm going to put on my rain boots and rain coat and kitchen gloves. And I'm going to leave the journal open on the kitchen table. Square in the middle. Even if I forget my own name, I won't be able to miss it. Here goes.

42.

Well, I'm back.

That wasn't the worst moment of my life but it sure made the top ten. The basement was dustier than I remembered. And I banged my elbow on just about every surface imaginable. I could hear water dripping somewhere, which was a whole lot of fun. But I didn't touch anything damp and

I got to the fuse box all right. I wasn't sure which fuses were blown so I changed them all. Except it didn't do anything. I was getting so scared I felt ready to throw up, so I climbed back out. I was halfway up the stairs when I realized there was no longer any orange glow filtering through the skylights.

So I guess it's finally happened. They cut the power.

43.

Maybe it really was a quarantine, and they've found a cure, and they're coming to get us.

44.

Or maybe they're finally pulling the plug.

45.

What do I do now? It feels so strange, just waiting around for what happens next. Like I was trying to land a damaged plane and it suddenly locked itself on autopilot and I don't know where this plane's going. I don't know if it's going to land or crash. All I can do is write because it's all I have. Like talking to someone. Serves no purpose but keeps my brain occupied. I keep holding my breath to hear better, and for the first time in who knows how long, I actually opened the windows despite the risks. But I can't hear a thing. Nothing but the rain.

46.

Checked the kitchen tap. There's still running water. I don't know what that means. I don't know if it means anything. Shit. Maybe they did cut off the water, but there's still some in the pipes. That makes sense, right? It's the only thing that makes sense. I'm going to leave it running for a while.

47.

Update. After five minutes the water was still running strong. I turned it off and closed all the windows again. Don't want amnesia mists filling up the house. Rereading the previous entries, I'm reassured. I remember them all. Still, I'd better keep going. Better write it all down. Everything that goes through my head. I cut off the water, but I can't cut off the rain. It's pouring. Sitting in the middle of the kitchen, writing in this journal with only my flashlight to see what I'm doing, I can hear it thrumming on the roof and tapping on the glass. Guzzling through the gutters and the drainpipes. It's like the house is digesting me.

48.

I should save my batteries but I don't know what else to do. I don't even know if I'll last the night. This journal's the only thing keeping me sane right now. If I stop just for one moment, the panic attack waiting at the edge of my mind will overwhelm me. My hands are shaking so much I can barely read what I've written. I wish I did have dementia. I wish I could forget forgetting. Like I did at first. When it was all just a confused haze. Days blurring into days. We didn't know there was something in the water. How could we? We didn't remember even a minute prior. We lived in a self-perpetuating present without past or future. There was no fear. I wish there was still no fear. Here I am thinking again of the Novocain and the razor blades and the warm bath and the sleeping pills. No pain. No fear. But I can't draw myself a warm bath because there's no power. A little bit of cold shouldn't be enough to stop me—and yet. The truth is you can't kill yourself when you're this scared of dying.

49.

Still listening, listening, listening. There won't be Novocain and razor blades, but I've decided. If I hear trucks outside, I'll go out bareheaded in the rain to meet them. And by the time they reach me I'll have forgotten to be scared. I can't hear any trucks, though. I still can't hear anything at all. Just the rain.

God. I'm writing in circles. I don't know what to do. I don't think there's anything I can do.

I'm going to close my eyes.

50.

There's something glowing in the bathroom.

51.

Oh God thank you God thank you Lord in heaven. Thank you so much. Jesus goddamn Christ and holy fucking hell.

52.

Calmed down by a fraction. Fucking Christ. I am such a stupid old woman. Thank you, God. I couldn't see the glow at first, because I kept turning the flashlight on and off to write and blinding myself with it. But after I closed my eyes, they got used to the dark and I saw the faint light from under the bathroom door. It so happens that the bathroom is the only room with a window to the back of the house, and the house backs up to Aloisville proper, down the hill.

If I'd only gotten up to walk from room to room, I could have noticed this *much* sooner, instead of sitting here shitting myself in the dark. Down the hill, all the way down, the lights are on. *The lights are on!* Nobody's cut the power lines. The town is safe. There's something wrong with my isolated neighborhood is all. Stupid, stupid old cow. Oh God. Thank you forever and ever.

53.

My hands have stopped shaking. My mind is clearer. The Army probably isn't coming into town to murder us all, but I have confirmed that my entire block is pitch black, including the street lights out the front door. Which must mean there's a problem with the electrical grid. It's a goddamn shame Katie visited me just yesterday. Her skills could have come in handy just now. But I've learned a few tricks of my own, and I can always ask her next week if I don't manage by myself.

54.

Damn it. Katie won't be here next week. She'll be dead, and her kid with her.

55.

Still shaken from those long minutes of bone-deep terror. The urge to write out my every thought has passed, though. I might as well try to sleep before dawn comes, which probably won't be for another couple of hours. Tomorrow, I'll go find Katie and ask her to help me. She won't be able to refuse. What is she going to do, run off and leave me powerless? No, she'll have to stop and help, and then I can convince her not to risk the life of her child. Hell. Maybe this grid problem is a godsend. I suppose I *was* wishing for a way to save Zoe.

And, well, if Katie doesn't listen to me and leaves without fixing my house, I can always move into hers. Much nicer than mine, and in a better neighborhood.

56.

Good morning.

Can't say I'm very proud of myself rereading what I wrote last night. But it's ballpoint pen; I won't be able to erase it. And I *was* in shock. Now it's dawn and my fear has passed. I have a battle plan—which I'd better write out in full—and motivation to the brim. Time to find the Rathbones before they go and get themselves mindwiped or worse.

I'll have to put on my rain suit. Guess what the weather's

like today! Welcome to Aloisville, rainiest town in the rainiest state. Population: we don't recall.

There's no real use waiting for it to stop. Even if it does, it'll always start again well before I'm done wandering the streets. So we put on armor and out we go. My outfit's not bad, if I do say so myself. Rain boots with two pairs of knee-high socks; hiking pants, the waterproof kind; a turtleneck, a balaclava and a windbreaker, with the hood up, the collar zipped, the strings tugged tight; and some swimming goggles to top it off. Add some rubber gloves, seal 'em with duct tape, and you're all set. Height of fashion, let me tell you.

Now, I have no blessed idea how I'm going to fix my lights, but if I have to get started anywhere, I figure Katie's house as good a place as any. Especially since she lives right across from City Hall, where they'll have a map of the electrical grid. That would be a big push in the right direction, for my sake and for Zoe's.

I'll keep my journal in my breast pocket, like always. It digs uncomfortably into my skin, but that way I always notice it's there.

Time to step outside. I've done this every other day since it all started, but I'm always afraid. Every time is like the first time—which is uncomfortably literal on the days I slip up and lose part of my memory. Today, though, I'm feeling enough anger and spite to pass for bravery. I'll be damned if I let Katie go through with her stupid plan. I'll be damned if I let my night of terror be for nothing. I'm off.

57.

So far so good. I had to take a break in Lilian Mason's house down the street. She's not here—got wiped long ago. Wandered out, leaving her door open, her French windows unbolted. Small mercies. It's a goddamn deluge out there, which brings on that mist I mentioned. I had to flip back a few pages to check that I had indeed mentioned it. My thoughts feel blurry. It's not a good day to be out, even by Aloisville standards.

In my experiments I roughed out a conversion equivalence, and I still recall it, which is good. A drop of rain will wipe the last ninety seconds from your memory. Could be more or less, depending on your weight and whether or not you're paying attention. The vapor hanging in the air can add up awfully quick. Gotta clear it from your lungs every few minutes, which is why I got my Nana's old oxygen bottle. Who knew it'd save my life fifteen years after she passed? Thank you, Nana. But I can't risk emptying it when I've barely left home, which is why I'm holed up at the Masons' now, waiting for the rain to thin.

My boots are caked in mud. This too can carry amnesia. The apocalypse is a weird thing: it means you can wipe your shoes on your dead neighbor's carpet and feel close to no guilt at all.

58.

Still raining hard. Lilian Mason used to do arts and crafts. Her last project is still sitting on her dinner table. Some godawful papier mâché house. But there's paper and pens and sheets of plastic, and it's giving me an idea.

59.

Should have written it down. Idiot. Should write everything down, especially when I'm out.

I pinned a note inside a plastic sheet to my chest, saying ELECTRICAL GRID. I guess I thought I'd just have to look down in case the mist got to me. Brilliant, right? Except it didn't work as well as I must have hoped. By the time I reached the heart of Aloisville, I couldn't remember what I was doing outside. I felt the sheet on my chest and looked down, but it wasn't any help. *Electrical grid.* What about it? Goddammit, Laverne, couldn't you write a complete goddamn sentence? Stupid old cow. But then I remembered the power was out at my house. Took me a while to make that connection, which meant my memory only goes back to the night before, now. Lost the whole morning already. Glad I wrote a bit in my journal earlier; it was nice to reread and *know.*

Had to take another pit stop in another abandoned house, to make sure I wouldn't get wiped any further. Now

I've learned my lesson, and I'm writing down my every last thought and action. At least I made it to town. The rain's calming down, too. My heart along with it. I've stopped taking breaths from my oxygen bottle. Water's just murmuring on the windows.

Sometimes I think about everything that's happening, really *think,* and I tell myself there is no explanation I'd accept. None.

Anyway, I've got an electrical grid to fix.

60.

Last pit stop, last house I'll break into today, hopefully. Needed a moment to calm down before the final stretch, because I nearly tripped on the uneven sidewalk. This is why you don't run in a rain outfit. It's so easy to slip and fall into a puddle. Rip your clothes, splash your hand in there, that's two or three days lost at once. Maybe even a whole week. And when you're confused you stay still and you lose more and more until you've got nothing left. It can happen so easily. I've seen it so many times. Baistach Hill and its empty children. Looking into those hollow eyes was the most frightening experience of my life. All the people in my nightmares have those same eyes now, no matter what the dream's about.

There's an umbrella in this house. Don't know whose it was but I'm going to borrow it, even though it's pretty much useless. The rain blows right under it, drips off the flaps, trickles down the shaft. In truly bad weather, an umbrella is actually more dangerous than nothing. But the streets get narrower close to City Hall, and people have stretched tarps over them. Like I said to Katie, I don't trust those plastic streets. Paranoia saves lives in Aloisville, which means it's not paranoia at all. I'm going to take this umbrella to walk under those tarps, and I'm not stopping 'til I reach City Hall.

61.

I'm getting real tired of things not working out.

It's not fair. I've come so far. On a truly rotten day, after a truly rotten night. The rain's stopped for now, which just feels ironic. I'm sitting on City Hall's front step because the door's locked—just my luck in this town full of open houses. I'm a tired old woman who just wishes things would be easy sometimes. I have to write this in case I forget what happened and need to remind myself all over again. Wouldn't be good for me. Aside from the obvious, my hip's aching these days, and I tend to lose my breath quicker than before. I made it here. But for what? The building's sturdy, with barred windows. I don't think I'll be able to break in.

I don't even have my balaclava over my face. I know it's insanely dangerous, but damn me, I can actually see the sun. The sun! I could weep, feeling this warmth on my skin. When the clouds close back in, I'll cover myself again. In the meantime I want to breathe. Just for a second.

62.

Damn it, God fucking damn it. I flipped back through the journal and realized I was supposed to go to Katie's house first, before trying City Hall. No matter what I find in here, won't be much help without an electrician at hand. And Katie and Zoe leaving on their foolish crusade! I forgot! It's been wiped away along with my morning and part of my night. I just sat here, with my goddamn empty mind, feeling sorry for myself, while they were right across the street. Their door's on the side, so they could have already left and I wouldn't have seen them. I have to go now. Damn it. I hope I'm not too late.

63.

Hold on. Just hold on for a minute.

Katie is an electrician. Katie lives right across from City Hall. Katie must have known I'd come here right away if my power went out. Gotta write this out. Gotta write it all. Wait. There she is. Katie's across the street. Carrying something looks like a bucket of wa

II

DAY ONE

It's been a strange day.

For me, it started when I came to my senses on the steps of City Hall, waking up slowly from the cotton haze of rain. Katie Rathbone was next to me. I was soaking wet. She said I'd stepped under a broken drainpipe. An empty red bucket was rolling away on the ground. If I'd only paid attention to it, I could have probably guessed heavy water was expected in the area. But I slipped up, walked straight into danger, and now I've lost bits of my life. How much? Who knows. That's what happens in Aloisville. I'm lucky Katie was there or I would've probably sat in the rain forever, thinning down to nothing.

At least I'm able to write it all down in my journal. The pages are a little damp, and I have to be careful not to rip them with my pen, but it's so much better than scrawling haphazard thoughts on the wallpaper like I used to do. Katie said she'd found it at my feet. I must have slipped it in my pocket right before leaving the house. I do feel an ache under my breast where it's been digging in. Shame I didn't write anything before I left. I wonder why it's been ripped in half. Must have done it myself, but why? Maybe I left the first half at my place for safekeeping.

The more I think about this morning, the more chilled I get. It could really have been the end of me. Katie was a wonder. We don't always see eye-to-eye, and she gets on my nerves most of the time, but in times of crisis, she's the one you want by your side. She kicked the bucket away—good thinking; those things are weapons of mass destruction here in Aloisville—and got me to follow her into her home across the street. Her little kid was there, quietly playing with markers. For a moment I didn't remember her name, and then it came back. Zoe. It's Zoe.

This I know.

As Katie got me to sit down, I noticed there was a note pinned to my chest in a plastic sheet. It said GO WITH KATIE RATHBONE, in handwriting so shaky it didn't even look like mine. Why did I write that? I do recall Katie and her daughter coming to visit the day before. Or maybe two days before. But I barely remember what we talked about; it's all a blur shortly after she got there. As always, the line between what's left and what's lost is muddled.

So this is my DAY ONE. I'm going to try to keep track of what happens to me as best I can. That way, if I walk under another drainpipe or stumble over a full bucket, I'll have something to fall back on. Gotta write it out. Gotta write it all.

I sat in Katie's living room waiting for my thoughts to fall back in line. I think I was staring into space for a long while, occasionally thumbing the sheet pinned to my chest, or blinking at little Zoe like I'd never seen a toddler before. Katie was endlessly patient, puttering around the house while she waited for my brain to pick up speed. Every once in a while, she would dab water off my hair so it wouldn't put pinpricks in my slowly re-inflating sense of self. Which is idiotic, really—once it's touched the body, rain loses its amnesiac charge. Even dead cells like hair or nails are no exception. When I batted her away, she chuckled and said I was beginning to act like myself again. God bless her, I suppose. She kept dabbing and I just had to let her, because without her it would've been much worse. She asked me again and again what I recalled. Couldn't quite blame her for being concerned about something like that. Probably trying to calculate how many hours I'd lost.

I didn't quite know what I remembered. Even as I write now, looking back on a day that easily could've been the last of my life, I still can't quite put it all together. Getting rained on is like losing a few pages in a book. You think you can figure out what's missing, because you know what happened before and what's happening now. But the truth is, you can never tell if what disappeared was crucial information or just filler.

When she asked me for the twelfth time or so, I lost my patience. Said I didn't remember anything and would she just stop asking? Which was when she cracked up laughing. Said she was hoping not to have to explain the plan again, but here we were. So she explained the plan. And when I called it stupid she said I mustn't mean that, since I'd de-cided to come, after all. *That* threw me for a loop.

At first, I didn't believe her. I told her she was talking nonsense. She just shrugged and took her kid in her arms before leaving the room, as if my objection didn't matter. As if she knew I was going to come around. So despite myself, I started really considering what she'd said. Me, agreeing to a suicide hike, after so many times of Katie asking and so many times of me telling her to go to hell? That didn't sound right at all.

But then I thought. What *else* would I be doing here? No-body in Aloisville goes out for a stroll anymore. Katie didn't force me into my rain outfit and drag me all the way down the hill, now, did she? And when I came back to myself, I was right across the street from her house. Obviously, I was coming to see her. Hell, the note pinned on my chest had her name on it, and I wasn't supposed to visit her for an-other week.

When I looked up, she was back with Zoe and an armful of child-sized rain clothes. That's when it really started to dawn on me. Katie and Zoe were about to try and leave town. And there was no doubt in Katie's mind that I was go-ing to join them.

I watched her dress Zoe up, with a little windbreaker and two pairs of pants, and plastic bags inside her socks, and frog-printed mini rain boots, and a scarf wrapped around her head, and woolen mitts and a woolen hat. I asked Katie if she had swimming goggles for the kid, and when she said no, I gave her mine. Zoe didn't like that and kept taking them off, which undid her scarf and knocked her hat askew. In the end I took the goggles back, just as Katie proclaimed us all ready to go. I wanted to argue against going. I'd argued against her a thousand times. But how could I argue against myself?

We went out, cautiously—it wasn't raining, though the clouds were threatening to spill any minute. We locked the door, which was something of a major event. Nobody locks their doors anymore in Aloisville; it's an unspoken rule that anybody should be able to run into any house, should the rain catch them off-guard. Katie must truly believe that nobody will need emergency shelter anymore—that everything is about to change.

She led the way to the southeast part of town, where the buildings are built close together and the alleys very narrow. Most of those streets are plastic streets, meaning they have tarps stretched overhead. Stupidly dangerous, I've always said so. She was bouncing Zoe in her arms, talking sweet nonsense to her. The kid was looking at everything with her big brown eyes. Too young to understand what we were doing or what her mother was saying, though she kept saying it: *we're going to see grandpa very soon, he's going to love you, yes he is.* That's when I snapped. *Katie,* I said, *you can't truly believe we're going to make it out of here. And I can't truly believe it either.* The look she gave me then—it reminded me all over again that we'd never been friends. She rolled her eyes and blew air through her nose and told me in that exasperated, high-pitched tone that this was a conversation she'd rather not have again. Tough goddamn luck, Rathbone. I told her she'd apparently convinced me once. So all she had to do now was convince me again. Was that so hard? Again with the superior air, adjusting her kid's weight in her arms. *Well I don't rightly know, Laverne*, she said. *You just turned up. I'm glad you did, because I couldn't bear the thought of leaving you alone up on that dreadful hill. But, tell you the truth, I never really understood what was going on in your tough old stubborn head, Laverne. My plan to eventually win you over was never about the plan itself, Laverne. It was about you and what you truly want, Laverne.*

What the hell does that mean, I ask you? Well, it shut me right up; not because it made an impression on me, but because it was so idiotic that I couldn't even think of a way to respond. Even now, writing down the day, I feel my teeth grinding again. Who died and made Katie Rathbone my goddamn spiritual advisor? There are no therapists in Aloisville, because all of them are about as traumatized and forgetful as the rest of us. I fumed about Katie's words for a mile of walking together. She kept cooing to her daughter in a cutesy voice. I thought to myself she'd be better off talking to her normally; that way the kid might start speaking in full sentences someday. But it didn't seem like a good time to snap at Katie, especially not when she'd saved my skin only a couple of hours before.

What I truly *want*. That one rattled around my head for a while. I kept trying and trying to remember what the hell I was thinking when I'd decided to tag along, but no dice. All I remembered was what my body remembered, which wasn't much. Only that I was hungry and tired and anxious, and that I'd probably been very afraid sometime in the past twenty-four hours, because my stomach didn't feel right and my nerves were shot up to hell. But this wasn't much help. I'm always afraid these days.

And then I thought: maybe that's why I agreed to go along with Katie's plan. So I'll finally stop being scared, one way or another.

Which led me into a passionate fit of self-loathing for the next mile or so. After everything, all my experiments and reconnaissance outings, all my efforts to survive and keep being myself in a town where mind bleach rains from the clouds, I suddenly decided to give up? I thought again about how my stomach and nerves bore traces of soul-rending terror. Something happened during the night, something that scared me so bad I . . . panicked and left to find Katie? Because I couldn't take the fear and the uncertainty anymore? I hate this theory because it makes sense. And I can't refute it, because I don't remember shit. All I have left is speculation. Have I been lying to myself thinking I didn't need people, didn't like them, even? Have I been secretly yearning for collective death rather than lonely survival? Because this is what it's going to be, no matter what Katie believes or pretends to believe. I might not remember the day before, but I remember the writing on my walls.

THEY SHOOT ON SIGHT. We don't know who the people at the borders are. What we do know is why they're here, and it's to keep us from getting out at all costs.

She pulled me into the school, a building I'd never set foot in, and I heard a rumbling of voices coming from the end of the hallway. A crowd. Not a big one, fifty people at most, but it still shook me to my core. The last time I'd seen more than two people in the same space was on Baistach Hill.

And just like that the memory of Baistach Hill overwhelmed me again. People turning from me because I'd euthanized children. Not looking me in the eye, even as they patted me on the back. They came to get me! Needed *me*! Who else was going to take care of those poor kids? Their parents? All of them empty, with nothing behind their eyes, so completely absent they were already dead. I did what had to be done because I was the only one who could do it. Even when I knew it would get me shunned, I made my peace with it. But now Katie Rathbone was leading me to a crowd, and I heard it from afar, all this noise, all this life.

My chest felt tight and my throat closed up and my eyes burned. All I could think was how badly I wanted to get out of Aloisville. I wanted to know if there was still a world out there. And so I walked into that room, even though I don't even *like* people, even though the old me would have never come in the first place. I walked in, behind Katie, and I stared at Zoe in her arms, and I thought of her growing up in this miserable tank of human suffering. I didn't even know any more if I believed the plan would work or if I just wanted to believe it. Didn't know if it mattered to me. Katie Rathbone had gotten into my head. *This is what I truly want,* I thought. *I want it to end.*

After that it gets blurry. People can be overwhelming when you haven't seen a lot of them in who knows how long. They didn't care that it was me, what with the atmosphere of generalized euphoria. On that day all sins were forgiven; all sinners welcome. I shook hands and gave nods. We all looked like circus freaks in our patched-up rain suits. I saw a man with a bike helmet, another wearing actual scuba gear, a woman stuffed in something made out of trash bags and duct tape. They were all laughing and chatting excitedly. That was the weirdest thing about them all. How cheerful they were. They didn't recoil when they heard my name. *Laverne!* some of them exclaimed. *My God! We haven't seen you in so long!* Have they all gone mad? I caught myself thinking maybe they didn't really remember me. Maybe they did what I didn't let myself do that day, and went to stand in the rain after we cleaned up Baistach Hill. Maybe I'm the only one left with those memories in my head.

Dave Logan was the star. He wore bright yellow rubber gloves and something like a neck brace over a police windbreaker. I saw him waving his phone around, yelling that there was still a world out there and soon the nightmare would end. Everyone was cheering and clapping at every word he said. Katie looked transported. Zoe looked anxious from the noise. I don't know what I looked like. The whole thing felt like a fever dream; not an outright nightmare but still too hot, too tight, the sense that something was wrong. Part of me wanted nothing more than to go to Dave Logan and shake him until he told me what goddamn day it was. If I only knew that, then I could die happy. But there was no chance in hell I'd ever reach him, surrounded as he was by his insane groupies. You would have thought they were all drunk. I even heard conversations about what we might do in the future with Aloisville's miraculous rain. Study it, use it for medical or military purposes, weaponize it. It was like we'd already made it out. For all these people, victory was a given. We could tell the world we were still here. We had a bargaining chip. We had leverage. We were powerful, we were unstoppable, we had the upper hand.

I started doubting myself again. Mostly because I wasn't buying into any of this. Walking through the crowd, all I could see were desperate fools who had gotten each other all worked up in their own little echo chamber. So deeply persuaded of their own ridiculous power. I wanted to yell at them to wake up. How did they know it was possible to bargain with the rubber people guarding the borders? Why did they think a single video would be enough to sway the guards? How were they so certain that the rest of the world—if it was still there—didn't *already* know we were here? They had no tangible proof. Only pipe dreams born out of exhaustion. I understand now why Katie has been so adamant from the start. She wants to buy what they're selling. And I have nothing against coping techniques. We all need illusions to survive. But the more I walked around, the clearer it became; this time the illusion had gone too far. The enthusiasm wasn't going to fall flat, like it had so many times before. Nobody could discourage these people, nobody could talk them out of their doomed plan; their hope was like a brick wall, and I could tell without a doubt that any skeptical word of mine would bounce right off. There were just too many of them.

I was done despising them. Now they were starting to scare me.

So I went to find Katie again, with my head screwed back on. I wanted to tell her I was leaving. It didn't matter how bad a night I'd had: morning had come. Whether or not I'd ever really come around to her way of thinking, I'd spun all the way back to the real me. I steeled myself for what she was going to tell me. I could hear it already. She would try to flip the script. She would say I was listening to my own fears and holding myself back. Too scared of the shadows to leave the cave. Choosing imprisonment and ignorance over bravery and freedom.

Except I was wrong. When I got to her, all she said was *there you are!* and gave me Zoe to hold, then vanished into the crowd. I didn't know where to go from there. I sat in a corner and gave the kid a page out of my journal, along with one of the pencils I'd taken from Katie's.

And then I wrote out the day in the hope that it'd help me make a choice. And now here I am.

*

I've reread my own entry five times already. Followed the course of my doubts, trailed by hope and fear. I saw myself thinking maybe I wanted to die, then deciding I really wanted to live. Here are my own thoughts all laid out, a reasoning that will not wash away in the rain, a thread I will be able to pick up even if I stumble under another drainpipe. Katie chooses hope over survival. I choose survival over freedom. But then I look at Zoe, and I don't know what to do. I've reread my own thoughts over and over until the words don't make sense. I look up, and Zoe is there, drawing on the page I gave her. And I still don't know what to do.

We are all going to sleep in the neighborhood homes tonight. In the morning, Dave Logan will lead his people to perdition. I have twelve hours left to change Katie's mind.

DAY TWO

Well, I slept the whole night, woke up too late in the morning, got into a screaming fight with Katie who called me a coward addicted to her own little comfort, and watched Dave Logan and all his people leave down the plastic streets. Several of them had children in their arms. They were singing and laughing, advertising where they were and how many they were and what they were doing. Zoe was looking at me over her mother's shoulder.

No, I didn't go. Hell. What was I going to do? Take her by force? At this point, Logan's people would have killed me. I know better than to antagonize a crowd. I tried to change their minds, these words as my witness. But they still left, and I left too, in the other direction. Away from the goddamn plastic streets, back home. Only to stop at Katie Rathbone's house. Walked around and got in through the kitchen. Now I'm going to stay here, waiting at the table, with the window open a little, until I hear gunshots. Only then will I leave for good.

Call it spite.

*

This kitchen is messy. Mud everywhere. She didn't even empty the trash. If I had gone away on a doomed journey I would have cleaned out my house top to bottom first. Like wearing clean underwear in case you get run over by a car and they cut off your clothes on the way to the ER.

I'd give anything to get run over by a car and be carried to the ER.

*

I'm waiting here. I'm just waiting. I'm not going back out there. I've decided. I'm only waiting to hear them die; sometimes there's nothing else you can do. When the gunshots begin they'll know I was listening. They'll know they're not dying alone. Or they won't know or care, because they'll be getting fucking shot at.

To hell with this. I'm going back home. I don't want to listen. I'm going back home.

*

I am still in Katie Rathbone's messy kitchen, and who the hell takes a kid with them on a march to death? Who the hell gets so deep into denial they'll bring their own child with them to the slaughter?

Goddamn Katie Rathbone and her goddamned daughter. I wish I had been paired up with anyone else. Anyone else at all.

Will these goddamn gunshots start already so I can leave this goddamn house?

*

If you're feeling bad for wishing people would get shot, Laverne, don't! You'll probably forget all about it on your way home.

*

I don't want to forget what they attempted. I don't want to forget they died. Even though I wish I could forget everything. Forget and start anew. If we could only start anew once we've been completely wiped then maybe everything would have been different. Maybe Aloisville would have been a paradise of innocence. Maybe that's how it was supposed to be.

*

Why is this kitchen so messy?

*

I'll repeat and underline it twice. *Why is this kitchen so messy?* I've been going insane, pacing the entire house, and everything else is spotless, tidy to a fault, just as I would've left it. You can tell Katie has been planning this for a long time. There was no way I could have made her change her mind. So why is the kitchen like this?

I'll tell you why. Writing this out is helping me think. It's because she had no time to clean it. It's because she messed it up yesterday, after she saved me from the rain. But she could have cleaned it afterwards. It's just a bit of mud and some trash to take out—you'd think that would be a problem, but honestly, we don't have a lot of trash anymore, and Aloisville's so empty we just pile it up on the edge of town and leave it.

If she didn't take out the trash, if she didn't clean the last bit of her house, then she couldn't. If she couldn't, it's because I was there. Because she was keeping an eye on me. To make sure I was fine. Right? To make sure I

I'm going to look in that goddamn trash can.

III

There's no DAY THREE, darling. Which shouldn't come as a surprise.

Doing daily entries was stupid anyway, considering the general situation. I should have gone for numbers instead. And that's what I did, at first. How nice to find myself in agreement with myself. Do you know what was in the trash can? Of course you do: the first half of the diary, the one I'm sure you've already read, because you like to do things in order. But back then I didn't have time to read it. The moment I found it is when I heard the gunshots at last.

So I just shoved it in my pocket and only opened it much later. By that time I had pieced together most of it anyway; finding it in the trash was enough to connect the dots. I still have some anger about that, I don't mind telling you. Who tosses half a person's brain away?

Yes, I pieced it together as I went back to the goddamn plastic streets. Wondering a hell of a lot about the bucket of water by the steps of City Hall, and Katie's timely arrival, and the way she bit her lip while she was dabbing the moisture from my hair, as if she felt guilty about something. Well, that's all I've got to say on the matter of Katie Rathbone's actions; as they say, you shouldn't speak ill of the dead. I suppose you can fill in the blanks for yourself. We're both so good at that.

Now you're wondering what happened next, and the truth is coming, if you want it. I'd rather you burn this whole journal, but I know you won't. I know what it's like to be starved for information, and I know that were I in your place, nothing could stop me from reading it all. Fair is fair, and I warned you.

So. Gunshots, right as I found the first half of the diary. I jumped, even though I was expecting them. They kept going, along with screams and the sound of a stampede. It was time for me to go home. I got up and took my bag and I didn't go home. I left the building and started heading after Dave Logan's idiots, because I'm an even greater fool.

If you asked me why, I couldn't give you an answer. A lifetime ago, I took an oath to do no harm. Does that still count when you're retired? It feels hypocritical to blame this noble idiocy on my profession.

The truth, darling, is that human life can be assigned a value, same as everything else. Before Logan's crowd left on their fool's errand, I weighed the value of all their lives and found it inferior to my own. I could have laid down in their path and refused to move. I could have forced them to remove me kicking and screaming, to tie me to a chair. They would have gone through with the plan anyway. All that for nothing, all that pain and humiliation for the same end result. So I didn't do it. Didn't even try. I could have left right away and safeguarded my ignorance; but I stayed close to the blockade as a form of revenge, waiting for those gun-shots, so I could say out loud *I told you so,* and then go back home knowing I was right, which is the thing people lust af-ter the most, even if they won't admit it.

So when I did finally hear them, I was stung by guilt and shame, and I suppose that is what propelled me forward, more than any true medical concern. Maybe I also didn't want Katie Rathbone to die, only so I could kill her myself. You will make up your own mind about mankind and what motivates us, but since I'm in the business of telling you the truth, I will say that in all of my remembered life I was never motivated by anything but myself. If I went to the block-ade, it was only so I could tell myself later that I hadn't just hung back and listened, that I'd tried to do something. Such is life.

And, well. I was thinking of you, too. Somewhere in the chaos of my mind.

When I got there, there wasn't a lot of panic in the street because the happy pioneers were dead already. It was driz-zling again; the air was cold enough that steam rose from the pools of blood. I told them the plastic streets were a bad idea. First of all, the tarps themselves are dangerous. Sec-ond of all, a narrow alleyway is not a good place to be when charging at a machine gun. They got mowed down easily. Fish, barrel.

As I stepped over the corpses, I kept thinking about how I'd come back to my childhood town for an easy retirement. Some peace and quiet with my loving husband. Life's got its own ideas, hasn't it?

Dave Logan was among the first I came across, which means the idiot ran away as soon as things went awry. Probably threw his own exalted followers behind him to shield himself. I could just about see him desperately trying to swim against the crowd, then getting trampled when they collectively began to panic. Studying his body, I realized he hadn't even died from a bullet wound. Some booted heel had crushed his windpipe. Ironic? Maybe. I threw up in a corner and kept going.

I could tell you about the other bodies I saw, most of them people I knew, but you get the idea. Even *I told you so* loses its flavor once you've puked a few times. I thought I'd seen it all, I thought nothing could shock me anymore, but right then I realized we were really nothing more than rabid animals waiting to be put down. I'd told Katie as much a thousand times but never believed I'd witness it myself. This long stretch of horror should have been nothing more than a funeral march, something I was planning to wipe from my own memory the very next day—this time, yes, I was going to do it. I was going to break my stupid stubborn streak of never giving myself voluntary amnesia. I had enough horrors in my mind for one life. But, of course, Aloisville chose that very moment to fuck me over one last time.

I saw movement up ahead. Survivors, I thought. Isn't it great being a doctor in the apocalypse? You think about what you *could* have done to help, if you'd only had the necessary supplies. Makes for real restful nights. But all the cynicism in the world couldn't have made me turn my back right then. You have to try. That's what some call the human condition, and what I call a goddamn curse.

The rain is what saved me, which is the kind of massive irony that makes me believe in a vengeful God. That thin white mist hanging in the air. I was motionless, which made me invisible, long enough to realize that the people lumbering towards me were not survivors of the stupidest march to freedom ever attempted. They were rubber guards coming into town.

I would have run away right there and then if not for the most acute panic attack of my life. It knocked the breath from my lungs and convinced me that I was in the line of fire; if I moved I would be spotted and shot down from afar. All I could do, when my knees began to give out, was pack myself behind a trash can, bring the lid down over me and stare through the holes in the rusted metal. I looked like a heap of trash myself, which probably helped.

That was the one good look I got at the border guards. They wore heavy boots and gas masks over their entire faces. Their whole bodies were black rubber, creaking as they walked. They were all armed with guns I didn't recognize. There was no convenient acronym stretched across their shoulders. They moved with purposeful strides and they didn't bother to step over the corpses, just trampled them. I hope you aren't looking for me to tell you who or what they were. I never even tried thinking about it afterwards; I've done enough of that for a lifetime. Does that outrage you? Will you call me incurious, cowardly, selfish? You're young, and I'm old, but that's not really an excuse. I've always been excellent at letting sleeping dogs lie.

They picked up some of the bodies. Piled them on stretchers. I could not tell you why, or according to what criteria. Some of their picks were still half-alive, some were fully dead. They took men and women, children and adults. Maybe they needed a representative sample. I didn't speak up to ask. As I huddled in the trash, curled up so tight it made my bad hip scream, I found myself wondering if this had happened before. I didn't know everything I'd seen; I didn't remember everything I knew. Perhaps I'd known the secret of Aloisville from the start and then forgotten it. Or perhaps all of Aloisville had seen something else, and then was made to forget. We'd been searching for the cause of the rain, never thinking the rain itself might be a consequence. The rubber guards marched into town and all I could think was: *this all happened before and will happen again.* People forget their own history, darling. Never needed the rain for that.

Was there ever something in the water? You'd think that's a stupid question, considering everything I've lived through, and everything I do remember. But the truth is I don't know. I don't know what happened and what I made up. I must be at least a little mad, so who's to say I'm not mad all the way? The truth is there is no truth. Only what we think we know.

Here is what I think I know:

The rubber guards walked past me, without seeing me, without coming to pick up the corpses next to me, which was dumb luck, pure and simple. There was almost a dozen of them, and they were entirely silent, though they seemed to be communicating. Thinking back, it made sense that they would use radio since they kept their faces entirely covered. At the time I did not make the connection; I only knew they were working together, according to a plan, towards a goal I couldn't understand. My mind and my body were still paralyzed with pure terror. Because I want to give you all the facts I will tell you I pissed myself and got scared they would hear it or smell it. But they walked past, and I was so out of my mind with fright it took me five entire minutes to realize what I was seeing.

The border was unguarded. The rubber guards were positive they had killed everyone, or at the very least chased everyone away. And the rain was pouring now, enough to deal with the survivors, despite the useless goddamn tarps. The mists were getting into my brain, enough to take the edge off the fear. All I saw was an open door, and all I thought was *God damn Katie Rathbone and God damn Dave Logan: I am about to prove them right.*

Coming into hope when you thought you had none— that's a strange form of folly. Dumb luck doesn't make for a good tale, and yet it's all I have to give you by way of an explanation. Dumb luck, laziness, and wrongful assumptions are the reasons I am able to write these lines today. I do believe they are the reasons behind a solid half of what happens on this Earth. If the rubber guards had only turned around, as I clumsily stumbled to my feet, I would have died. If only one of them had trailed behind, or finished their job early, I would have died. If I had stepped on something that had cracked or snapped under my foot, I would have died.

I limped blindly towards the barricade, walking right in the middle of the street, too dazed to even try to hide my progress. The rain thrummed on the tarps overhead, pounding furiously in hopes to get me, and that too was luck, because it muffled all the noise I was making. The water was falling in a sheet where the tarps ended, a few dozen feet before the dark mass of the blockade. Through that glass curtain, I could see the machine guns resting quietly in their turrets, oddly deformed by the moving water. How is it possible, I wonder now, that none of the rubber men had stayed behind to guard the border? Not a single one? After keeping such an airtight lock on our miserable town for God knows how long, why had they slipped up now? And once again, the answer: dumb luck, laziness, and wrongful assumptions. We all subsist on each other's mistakes, darling. They are the atoms of our own success.

It was raining so hard I couldn't see much of anything beyond the blockade, except for a stretch of cracked concrete path disappearing into sparse woods. Such a trite glimpse, yet it was the highway to heaven. Remember, now, that Aloisville was my childhood home. I knew exactly where that road led. I knew its bends and curves by heart. I knew the fields beyond, I knew where to hide and where to find water, what hill to keep in front of me if I wanted to reach the main road undetected. If I only made it past the finish line, if I could perform the miracle of remaining unnoticed for a minute longer, I could vanish into the countryside where no one would ever find me. As I walked—my eyes still full of all the blood I was seeing, my guts still twisting with abject fear—as I walked, hope filled my heart like a blazing sun and burned up all the rest. I had never felt anything like it, and I never will again. The mists kept erasing the last few seconds from my mind, so I never ran out of awe. Each moment was the same epiphany on a loop. It was like glory made solid with every breath. I was going to leave Aloisville forever. The thought swelled into my brain, seeped into my marrow, became part of my bones. I knew it for certain.

This, of course, is where you come in.

At the last moment, right before I stepped through that damned sheet of rain—I was hesitating, even in my frenzied state; it was uneven, I was covered up, I would probably be fine, but how to be sure?—I saw you. Huddling in a ball. And you're thinking now, reading these words: *here is the part where she saves me.*

But again, this is a story about dumb luck. You are lucky: I was out of my mind with an emotion too huge to have a name. You are lucky: I was not able to pick the reasonable option. You are lucky: my hindbrain remembered I'd been looking for you. I would have left you there, if I had only been able to think rationally. But I could think about nothing. My mind was an eternal present, a self-repeating thought. Everything that can happen must happen, it seemed to me. And here you were. So I limped over to you and picked you up. You were shaking and hiccupping; the noise of the machine guns, more than anything else, must have scared you. Other than those wet, crushed sobs, you were quiet. You had always been quiet, which is the only explanation I can offer for the rubber guards passing you by, just as they had passed me by. Or maybe they saw how young you were and figured the problem would sort itself out.

In that moment my illumination of glory had not yet vanished. I'd gone in to find you, after all; there you were, miraculously spared. Everything was going so very well. It was a complete and utter moral victory for me. The universe had designated me as its heroine and prophetess. All of Aloisville, it seemed, had been a setup for my big moment. Isn't it easy to be the hero at the right time, in the right place?

I held you tight against me, so tight you almost cried out, struggling for a moment in my grip. I was drunk on mild amnesia, endorphins, and shock. It was a formidable few seconds.

I could end the story here. I've debated doing just that, while sitting here at my desk, smoking—I recommend taking up bad habits in your old age—writing through the night, stopping every once in a while to think and stare at the ceiling. But I think I want you to know everything. Not because you deserve to know; I don't quite think anybody deserves anything in this world—and I mean that in the least malicious way imaginable, darling. Almost with fondness really. Not because you *should* know, either; I have no doubt these lines are going to upset you deeply. I'm not sure what you think of me on the best of days, but I've always known, myself, that I'm not a kind person. Someone kind wouldn't have given you the first half of the journal to read, much less the second half; a kind person certainly would not have written this account so you could know the rest. If I am telling you the truth, well, it's because the truth is greater than us both. It is the horizon we must strive to reach, even though it is an illusion—even more so in my case, what with all the rain sloshing around in my head. Do I sound dramatic? Perhaps, darling. It's what happens when I remember that day, when I felt like I was at the glorious center of the universe, and how Katie fucking Rathbone brought it all *crashing down.*

She limped out of her own hiding spot. Will you believe it? She hadn't taken a single bullet, not a one. Like Dave Logan, the crowd had caused all of her wounds. She had lost most of her protective gear, and I could see that her hair was matted with blood. I could also tell, by the way she looked at me, that she hated me with a burning, animal passion. I don't think anybody will ever hate me the way she did then. I suppose we all have our own narratives in our heads. Maybe I was a bad luck charm in Katie's understanding of things; after all, I'd predicted doom and stayed behind while they all went ahead to get shot. And here I was now, swooping in to steal their victory, after they'd all obligingly paved the road in blood. Seeing her brought up no particular emotion inside me, only a vague confusion and an unfortunate impulse to say again *I told you so.* I was right. Hadn't the universe made it clear? By definition, she had to try and ruin it for me. She couldn't let me get away with it, not when I was so undeserving of it, in her own warped version of events.

Give me back my child, she said. Then she called me a word I will not write here; my commitment to facts has its limits. All I could think was: *I knew I didn't like the bitch.* Even in the depths of my own trance, it was clear to me that she was too livid to understand we could have all three escaped. She didn't see the path to freedom stretching behind me. All she saw was that I was alive and well, that you were in my arms, and that it was *unfair,* because *she* should have been rewarded for the pain and death of her fallen comrades.

She said it again. *Give me back my child.* Which is when I gave into some idiocy of my own. What I should have done, obviously, was turn around and walk away. She would have followed, black and blue and staggering, and once we were both safe and out of town, far enough that no one could find us, we could hash it out. Have a shouting match, hit each other a few times. Probably come to an understanding based on your safety. But instead—because I was *right,* and I wanted her to admit I had been right from the very start—I stood there and tried to convince her to shut up and follow me. As if we had ever managed to convince each other of anything. *We have to go,* I said. *Katie, we have to go. Don't you understand?*—and so on and so forth. It was obvious she couldn't understand me, and didn't care to try. All she cared about was that you were in my arms. *Give me back my child*—and I realized right then I'd lost my chance to walk away. If I did that now, she would keep screaming and screaming until the rubber guards finally caught on, deaf bastards, and came back to kill all three of us.

Another option crossed my mind: to give her what she wanted. Put you on the ground and leave. If she followed, good; if she didn't, too bad for you both. But you see, the truth is not wholly awful. Even though I considered it, I couldn't abandon you. I liked you. You looked so much like me. You could have been my granddaughter. You were going to be my granddaughter. Katie was limping forward now, reaching out, letting out incoherent noises. Maybe her head wound was worse than I thought.

I saw it begin to happen.

I couldn't have prevented it. That's what I tell myself. All I could think was that, yet *again,* I had been right. But it didn't feel good anymore; it was beginning to feel like a punishment. Still, when I think back on it—how many *times* had I told her the plastic streets were a bad idea? How many times had I told her the tarps were a hazard?

She stepped forward just as the oilcloth overhead bent and gave under the weight of the rain. A pregnant belly that just couldn't wait any longer. Gallons of rainwater splashed over Katie, who was bareheaded with her collar open, without gloves, without even a windbreaker, having lost them all during the mad struggle, the terrified mob pushing against her, trampling her almost to death. She opened her mouth wide and screwed her eyes shut. It must have been really cold. Rainwater trickled down her jaw, dribbled down her chin, plastered her hair to her face.

Little sugar doll. I knew, the second she opened her eyes. Empty inside: got her all in one.

It's what I remember still, about this awful day I didn't get a chance to forget. All those corpses I saw, all the blood and the bodies—and yet she is what I dream about at night, when you hear me scream and come to my room asking what's wrong. It's your mother's eyes with nothing behind them; it's a human mind dissolved in seconds of pouring water, trickling away into puddles, swallowed by the sewers, returned to the sea. It's the body without a soul, swaying there, no longer screaming, no longer doing or thinking or being anything.

Is this why you should hate me? You decide. At this point in time, you might still be on the fence. Read on, darling. I know you will. You want to know, because I gave you my stubbornness.

I left her there. And as I walked away, past the blockade, up the dirt road, into the woods, I didn't turn back to look at her once. For all that she haunts me now, I wasn't crying then. Good riddance, I thought. Noisy bitch trying to get us killed. Wouldn't listen to reason. Nasty thoughts, but it was like someone else was thinking them for me. I didn't feel anything like anger or vindication to back them up. I didn't feel much of anything. My moment of crazed glory was gone; my thoughts were a series of actions to execute. Maybe I was in shock. I remember that my hip hurt from hiding in the trash, and it was bothering me to the point that I couldn't think about much else. I remember you were heavier than I'd imagined, and I didn't know how to hold you right.

The mistake I made was allowing you to see over my shoulder. Your first word—the first I heard, in any case— was *no!*

Sharp and piercing. At this point I didn't think you *could* make any noise. I startled so badly I almost dropped you. *No! No! No!* you were shrieking, and wriggling and kicking, and then *Mama! Mama! Mama!* Wailing, struggling, trying your damnedest to get me to put you down. You almost got us killed, Zoe. You were so goddamn loud. Me, I knew those woods. I knew those fields. I was confident I could reach a safe place. You looked like me, enough that nobody would even think of asking questions. Unless you were screaming for your mother.

It was still pouring, and you were very young, so three minutes in the rain was enough to do the trick.

Acknowledgments

Thank you, Troix, for fishing me out of the pile; without you, who knows where I'd be?

Thank you, Carl and Matt, for your faith and your enthusiasm; I am so glad you were my first editors.

Thank you, Irene, Jackie, Jeff, Lauren, Nadav, Christine, Andrew, Ashley, Mary Louise, Jessica, and everyone else at Tordotcom; I've not met you, yet you've carried me.

Thank you, Mom and Dad and Bro, for reading me in either language; I love you in both.

Thank you, Thon and Boa, my best and oldest friends; I knew you'd complain if I didn't mention you anywhere.

Thank you, my seven beloved pocket people; next time, the castle is yours.

About the Author

NAOMI SALMAN is a writer, editor, and translator. She has published fiction in both French and English, and been nominated for a Prix du Jeune Écrivain and an Eisner Award. She lives and works in Paris. *Nothing but the Rain* is her first novella.

TOR·COM

Science fiction. Fantasy. The universe.

And related subjects.

*

More than just a publisher's website, *Tor.com*

is a venue for **original fiction, comics,** and

discussion of the entire field of SF and fantasy,

in all media and from all sources. Visit our site

today—and join the conversation yourself.